A NOTE TO PARENTS

Reading Aloud with Your Child
Research shows that reading books aloud is the single most valuable support parents can provide in helping children learn to read.
- Be a ham! The more enthusiasm you display, the more your child will enjoy the book.
- Run your finger underneath the words as you read to signal that the print carries the story.
- Leave time for examining the illustrations more closely; encourage your child to find things in the pictures.
- Invite your youngster to join in whenever there's a repeated phrase in the text.
- Link up events in the book with similar events in your child's life.
- If your child asks a question, stop and answer it. The book can be a means to learning more about your child's thoughts.

Listening to Your Child Read Aloud
The support of your attention and praise is absolutely crucial to your child's continuing efforts to learn to read.
- If your child is learning to read and asks for a word, give it immediately so that the meaning of the story is not interrupted. DO NOT ask your child to sound out the word.
- On the other hand, if your child initiates the act of sounding out, don't intervene.
- If your child is reading along and makes what is called a miscue, listen for the sense of the miscue. If the word "road" is substituted for the word "street," for instance, no meaning is lost. Don't stop the reading for a correction.
- If the miscue makes no sense (for example, "horse" for "house"), ask your child to reread the sentence because you're not sure you understand what's just been read.
- Above all else, enjoy your child's growing command of print and make sure you give lots of praise. *You are your child's first teacher — and the most important one. Praise from you is critical for further risk-taking and learning.*

— Priscilla Lynch
Ph.D., New York University
Educational Consultant

D0017414

To Edie,
who always makes me look good!
— G.M.

For Ruth,
the greatest storyteller of them all
—J.S.

Text copyright © 1995 by Grace Maccarone.
Illustrations copyright © 1995 by Jeffrey Scherer.
All rights reserved. Published by Scholastic Inc.
HELLO READER!, CARTWHEEL BOOKS, and the CARTWHEEL BOOKS
logo are registered trademarks of Scholastic Inc.

Library of Congress Cataloging-in-Publication Data
Maccarone, Grace.
    "What is that?" said the cat / by Grace Maccarone;
    illustrated by Jeffrey Scherer.
        p.   cm. — (Hello reader! Level 1)
    "Cartwheel Books."
    Summary: An assortment of animals tries different ways to get a big box
open, only to be VERY surprised by what is inside.
    ISBN 0-590-25945-8
    [1. Animals—Fiction.   2. Stories in rhyme.]
    I. Scherer, Jeffrey, ill.   II. Title.   III. Series.
    PZ8.3.M127Wh   1995
    [E]—dc20   94-39100
                                                    CIP
                                                    AC

12 11 10 9 8   9/9 0/0

Printed in the U.S.A.   23

First Scholastic printing, October 1995

"What Is THAT?" Said the Cat

by Grace Maccarone
Illustrated by Jeffrey Scherer

Hello Reader! — Level 1

SCHOLASTIC INC.
Cartwheel B·O·O·K·S ®
New York Toronto London Auckland Sydney

"I found a box," said the fox.

"I heard," said the bird.

"What is that?"
said the cat.

"We don't know," said the crow.

"It is big," said the pig.
"Let me see," said the bee.

 z z z

"Open it up," said the pup.
"How?" said the cow.

"I'll use force,"
said the horse.

"Use a bat," said the rat.
"I will try," said the fly.

"Good luck," said the duck.
"Beware!" said the hare.

CLICK

DO
NOT
OPEN

Then

the fox

and the bird

and the cat

and the crow

and the pig

and the bee

and the pup

and the cow

and the horse

and the rat

and the fly

and the duck

and the hare

said,

"See you later,

alligator!"